# Dragons Don't
# Cook Pi...

Check out all the books about

# The
# BAILEY SCHOOL KIDS

ISBN-13: 978-0-590-84904-3
ISBN-10: 0-590-84904-2

40 39 38 37 36 35 34 33 32                    8 9 10 11 12/0

Printed in the U.S.A.                    40

This edition first printing, July 2007

Book design by Laurie Williams

# Dragons Don't Cook Pizza

by **Debbie Dadey**
and
**Marcia Thornton Jones**

**illustrated by John Steven Gurney**

Scholastic Inc.

New York Toronto London Auckland Sydney
Mexico City New Delhi Hong Kong Buenos Aires

*To my husband, Stephen Walter Jones,
because he never turns into a dragon on
all those pizza dinner nights!*
—MTJ

*For Nathan and Becky Dadey—
my favorite pizza eaters.*
—DD

# Contents

# 1

## Pizza

"Yippee!" Eddie yelled as he jumped off the bus and ran toward Jewel's Pizza Castle. Eddie and the rest of the Bailey School third-graders were on a field trip to the newest pizza place in town.

Even though it was a new building, it looked a thousand years old. The walls reminded Eddie of gray mold on bread, and the flags waving from the four corner turrets were faded with age. A splintery drawbridge led to the front door. Eddie couldn't wait to thunder across it, but he skidded to a stop when Mrs. Jeepers stepped in front of him.

Mrs. Jeepers was Eddie's teacher and she didn't put up with yelling. She didn't put up with any mischief. She was so strict and so strange that some kids

1

thought she was a vampire. "Eddie," Mrs. Jeepers said in her Transylvanian accent. "That will be quite enough running and shouting. I expect you to behave."

Eddie nodded and Mrs. Jeepers quickly lined the students up to go into the pizza parlor. Eddie went to the back of the line with his friends Howie, Melody, and Liza.

"Mrs. Jeepers never lets us have any fun," Eddie complained.

"Sure she does," Liza said, pulling a hat over her blond hair. "No other teacher ever brought us to Jewel's Pizza Castle."

"Big whoop, we had to read a million books just to be able to go," Eddie grumbled. "Then we can't even yell or run. What's so fun about that?"

"They have video machines and double deluxe pizza," Howie said.

Melody followed her class up to the gray castle-like building. "I can't wait to

sink my teeth into a big slice of pepperoni. That'll make reading all those books worth it."

"I had fun reading," Liza admitted.

Eddie pulled his baseball cap off and bopped Liza over the head. "Earth to Liza — are you there? Are you still in the Dark Ages? Reading is only fun when there are monsters and supersonic airplanes involved. Those books Mrs. Jeepers made us read were definitely not fun!"

"I liked them," Howie argued.

"Me, too," Melody said. "But I'm ready to eat pizza!"

The kids trampled across the drawbridge and squeezed inside the heavy wooden door. They ran smack dab into the oldest, wrinkliest man they had ever seen.

"Yikes!" Liza squealed.

# 2

## The Dragon's Lair

"Welcome to Jewel's Pizza Castle," the old man said. "I am George, the ruler of this pizza kingdom." He had a pointy beard and spoke in a low voice that came from deep inside his chest.

"Thank you," Mrs. Jeepers said. "These students earned a pizza party by being reading wizards." She smiled her odd little half-smile and looked at the third-graders from Bailey Elementary School.

"Every castle needs wizards," George said. "Please come in." George led them into the dingy pizza parlor and past several small eating rooms. Above the door to each room was a sign written in fancy letters. He stopped at the entrance to a large room. The sign over the door said

*The Dragon's Lair.* Beneath the sign was a shiny sword.

"This is the main dining hall," he told Mrs. Jeepers. When he disappeared through two swinging doors at the end of the room, all the kids scrambled to find a place at the long tables.

"This is the strangest pizza place I've ever been to," Liza said.

Melody nodded. "It's so dark."

"Maybe George is trying to hide dirty

floors," Eddie said with a laugh.

Howie ignored his friend's joke. "It's supposed to be like a castle of long ago," he told his friends.

"I'm pretty sure kings and queens never ate pizza," Melody said.

"Maybe not," Howie told her. "But I think the castle idea is fun."

Just then, two servers barged through the swinging doors. The sign over the swinging doors said *Dungeon*. "My grandmother would like this place,"

Eddie said. "She thinks kitchens are dungeons, too."

The servers placed silverware, napkins, and water glasses in front of all the students and Mrs. Jeepers. The napkins were covered with fancy letters. One of the servers was dressed in a long peasant dress and the other wore a vest that looked like armor.

"Great," Eddie joked. "Now all we need is a knight on horseback and a fire-breathing dragon."

Just then a deep rumble shook the silverware.

A girl named Carey screamed and a few kids whimpered. They all looked at their teacher. Mrs. Jeepers' green eyes flashed in the direction of the swinging doors and her fingers touched the magic brooch she always wore at her throat.

"What was that?" Liza whispered.

"I think it was Mrs. Jeepers' stomach growling," Eddie joked. But he stopped laughing when another rumble made their water glasses dance across the table. When the rumbling stopped, a cloud of smoke rolled through the crack of the swinging doors.

# 3

# The Dungeon

"Fire!" Melody gasped.

But before anybody could scramble from their seats, George pushed through the swinging doors and smiled at the Bailey School kids. "No need to worry," he said in his deep voice. "I have taken care of the . . . problem."

"Perhaps we should leave and come back another day," Mrs. Jeepers suggested.

George tugged at his pointy little beard and shook his head. "Please stay. It was just my special pizza cook. Sometimes he gets a little cranky when things don't go right. But I have convinced him to settle down."

"If you are sure everything is all right," Mrs. Jeepers said.

"I am very sure," George told her. "And you will be glad you stayed. Our pizza chef is the best in all of Bailey City."

By the time the kids ate their lunch, they knew George was right. "This is the cheesiest pizza I've ever had," Melody said.

"I don't care if he does have dirty floors," Eddie said. "Jewel's Pizza Castle makes the best pizza around." He reached for the last piece of pizza, but a boy named Huey grabbed it first.

"I wanted that!" Eddie yelled.

"Too bad," Huey said as he sank his teeth into a piece of pepperoni.

"No fair," Eddie grumbled.

"Maybe George will tell us his secret ingredients," Liza said. "Then we can make pizza just like it at home."

But when Liza asked, George quickly shook his head and the blood drained from his face. "Our pizza chef guards his recipes as if they were treasures."

"Then perhaps my students could take a tour of your kitchen," Mrs. Jeepers suggested.

George backed away from the table until he was against the swinging doors. No one could go in or out. When George spoke, his deep voice shook. "A tour of our kitchen is not possible. Maybe some other time." Then George disappeared through the swinging doors.

The rest of the third-graders grabbed their coats and hurried to line up behind Mrs. Jeepers. They slowly filed out of *The Dragon's Lair* dining room. But Melody, Liza, Howie, and Eddie stayed behind.

"What's in that kitchen he doesn't want us to see?" Melody asked quietly.

"I told you," Eddie said. "Dirty floors!"

"No," Howie said. "There's something much worse than dirty floors."

"Maybe he's holding Jewel's Pizza Cas-

tle's king and queen prisoner," Liza said. "After all, the sign over the kitchen door does say it's the dungeon."

"He could be hiding a dragon," Melody teased. "That would explain all that growling and the smoke."

Liza giggled and Eddie laughed out loud. But not Howie. His eyes grew round and his mouth dropped open.

"What's wrong with you?" Melody asked.

"That pizza gave him heartburn," Eddie said. He grabbed Howie's elbow and pulled him after the rest of the third-graders. But they hadn't gone far when Melody stopped dead in her tracks.

"That's odd," Melody said.

"What?" Eddie asked.

Melody pointed to the empty spot over the door to *The Dragon's Lair*. "I'm sure there was a sword hanging under that sign when we went in."

"Melody's right," Howie said. "I saw it, too."

"Then where is it now?" Liza asked.

"I have an idea," Howie said slowly. "But I don't think you're going to like it!"

# 4

# Dragons for Dinner

Howie waited until they were back on the bus to talk. He checked to make sure no one else was listening. All around him kids were talking, laughing, and singing. Howie huddled close to Liza, Eddie, and Melody.

"What's this all about?" Eddie asked.

"You'll probably laugh," Howie said.

Eddie shrugged. "Only if what you say is stupid."

"Come on and tell us," Melody said, "before my pigtails turn gray."

"All right," Howie said, "but first I want to tell you about a book my mother read to me once."

Eddie rolled his eyes. "Oh, brother. I'm being haunted by books!"

"You would like this one," Howie told

his friend. "It's about a ferocious monster and the man who captured it."

"Now you're talking," Eddie said. "What kind of monster was it?"

Howie paused, then softly he said, "A dragon."

Eddie laughed and slapped Howie on the back. "Poor Howie, how can someone be so smart in math and so dumb in life?"

"In real life," Melody said softly, "there are no such things as dragons."

"I'm not dumb and I know about real life," Howie snapped. "I think that George took that sword down to control a dragon, just like in my story."

"That would be mean," Liza said.

"Hold your horses," Eddie said. "First of all, there is no dragon. But if there were, everybody knows that swords are the only way to control dragons."

"Being mean is no way to control anything," Liza said.

"Oh, yeah?" Eddie said, putting his fist in the air.

"Whoa," Melody said, pushing Liza and Eddie back into their bus seats. "Let's not get carried away. Remember, there is no dragon. Howie was just kidding around. After all, what would a dragon be doing in Bailey City?"

Eddie nodded as the bus started up. "Right. I'm pretty sure that dragons don't cook pizza, and they definitely aren't chefs at rinky-dink pizza joints."

Suddenly the bus started shaking and a loud rumbling filled the air. The kids grabbed onto their seats. "What's going on?" Liza squealed.

"Either our bus is going to blow up or Eddie made the dragon mad!" Howie screamed.

"I never thought that I'd be so happy to go back to school!" Liza yelled.

The kids gripped the seats and held on for the ride of their lives.

# 5

## Bad Breath

"Roar! ROAR!" Eddie jumped out at his friends from behind the oak tree on the school playground.

"Very funny, Eddie," Liza said. "You're the scariest dragon I've ever seen."

"Or ever will see," Eddie told her as he took off his green dragon hat. Eddie had stapled green paper scales and a big snout to his baseball cap. He was trying to scare his friends. It was the morning after their pizza party and it was almost time for school to start. "Dragons don't exist," Eddie said, fixing the scales on his hat.

"Just because you've never seen one, doesn't mean they don't exist," Melody said.

"If we ever do see one," Howie told

Eddie, "I bet his breath won't smell as bad as yours."

"Dragons breathe fire all the time," Liza said matter-of-factly. "Of course they'd have bad breath."

"Then what's your excuse for bad breath?" Melody giggled and poked Eddie in the chest.

"Eddie may have dragon breath," Liza interrupted, "but I'm afraid he doesn't know riddles like a real dragon does."

"What is she talking about?" Eddie asked.

Howie reached into his coat pocket and pulled out a tattered piece of paper napkin. "Dragons are famous for telling hard-to-solve riddles," Howie explained. "Like this one we got at Jewel's Pizza Castle."

"I didn't get a riddle," Eddie said.

"I got one," Melody said.

"Me, too," Liza said. "But I couldn't figure it out." Liza and Melody pulled crumpled napkins from their coat pockets.

"Mine was really hard," Melody said. Then she read her riddle out loud:

Inside me deep
There is much heat
Captured sadness
Lonely madness
My only joy
To cook for girls and boys

"That's what mine says," Liza said.

Howie nodded. "Mine, too,"

"Why didn't I get one?" Eddie asked.

"You probably did," Howie said, "but you were too busy making a paper airplane to notice. Or maybe George figured riddles weren't for you."

"Are you saying I'm not smart enough to figure out some stupid dragon riddle?" Eddie said, snatching Liza's paper. "I'm smarter than any dragon and I can prove it."

Liza shivered as Eddie unwrapped the riddle. In the distance, she was sure she heard real roaring. It was just like the strange sound they'd heard yesterday at Jewel's Pizza Castle.

# 6

## Dead Serious

Tiny snowflakes landed on the paper as Eddie stared at the riddle. Liza shivered again when the cold wind rattled the bare branches over her head. Howie stuck his hands under his arms to keep them warm.

"I've got it!" Eddie yelled.

"What?" Melody asked. "Cooties?"

"No, pizza brains," Eddie snapped. "I've figured out the answer to your riddle." Eddie looked like he'd just won a battle. "And you said I wasn't smart enough to solve riddles!"

Howie patted Eddie on the shoulder. "We didn't mean it," Howie said. "Now, tell us the answer."

Eddie puffed up his chest. "It's obvious. Just look at the first two lines and the an-

swer will be as plain as the pepperoni on George's pizza."

Melody unfolded her riddle and read out loud:

"Inside me deep,
There is much heat."

Liza, Melody, and Howie stared at the paper for a full minute before Liza shrugged. "I still don't get it," she said.

"Now who's stupid?" Eddie asked with a grin.

"We take it all back," Melody said. "Just tell us the answer."

"Please?" Liza added.

"Well," Eddie said. "Since you're my best friends, I guess I can share my endless wisdom with you."

"Just TELL us!" his three friends yelled at once.

"Okay, okay," Eddie said. "Don't go getting your shorts ruffled. The answer is . . . an oven!"

"An OVEN!" Howie yelled. "That's the silliest thing I ever heard."

"Wait," Melody said. "It does fit. A pizza oven is deep. Like a cave. And the last line of the riddle talks about cooking."

"But ovens aren't lonely or captured," Howie pointed out.

"Then you come up with an answer," Eddie told his best friend.

Howie nodded. He looked at each of his friends before he said a word. "I have an answer," he said finally. "I've thought about it all night. It's the only answer that fits all the clues."

"What is it?" Melody asked. "What's the answer?"

Howie motioned his three friends closer. When he spoke, his voice sounded serious. "The answer," he said, "is a dragon."

Eddie slapped his forehead. "Would you quit yapping about your make-believe dragon and get serious?"

"I am serious. Dead serious," Howie said. "And I think these slips of paper are more than silly riddles. Much more. I believe they're cries for help."

"Who would try to get help by putting riddles onto paper napkins?" Liza asked.

"There's a dragon in George's dungeon," Howie explained, "and he's begging us to free him. It's up to us to help him."

# 7

# More Than Make-Believe

"Duck!" Eddie yelled before Howie could say another word. "There goes a wild dragon now!"

Eddie flapped his hat all around Howie's head before Howie grabbed the dragon hat and glared at Eddie. "Go ahead and make jokes. But I know all

about dragons, and they're more than make-believe."

"How can you be so sure?" Liza asked.

"Once, in the days of kings and castles, knights made their fortunes battling fire-breathing monsters. These horrible beasts terrorized people by breathing fire on the crops and eating up young girls."

"Sound like the perfect house pets to me," Eddie said with a grin.

Melody jabbed her elbow into Eddie's side, but Howie continued his story.

"The knights destroyed all the dragons, except for one. It was the most dangerous dragon of them all," Howie told his friends. "Knight after knight rode off to battle the terrible beast, but they never returned."

"What happened to them?" Liza asked in a whisper.

"The dragon gobbled them up," Howie told her. "So the king sent for the most famous knight of all. He was known throughout the land because his magic sword could hypnotize even the most savage of dragons. That knight's name was St. George."

Liza gasped and Melody's eyes grew round. "That's the restaurant owner's name," Melody said.

Howie nodded. "Exactly. George of Jewel's Pizza Castle is the one and only St. George the dragon tamer."

"But why didn't St. George kill the last dragon?" Melody asked.

"Because a dragon's scales hold the secret to eternal life," Howie told her. "St. George tamed that ferocious beast so he could live forever. Now he's keeping his fire-breathing dragon captive in Bailey City and using its fire to bake pizza." Howie waved his mysterious riddle under his friends' noses. "And the dragon has had enough."

Liza looked at Howie's riddle and

sniffed. "If Howie's right, then that dragon must be the saddest creature alive."

Melody nodded. "That's exactly what the riddle says." She read the middle two lines of the riddle out loud:

"Captured sadness,
Lonely madness."

Howie stood up tall and nodded. "It's up to us to free the dragon!"

Eddie laughed so hard he fell back against the trunk of the giant oak tree. "Howie's lost it now," Eddie said. "He's trying to convince us to jailbreak a make-believe monster."

"Maybe Eddie's right," Melody said. "After all, dragons live in fairy tales, not Bailey City."

"They guard treasure and cook fair maidens for dinner," Eddie added.

Liza nodded. "And I'm pretty sure dragons don't cook pizza," she said.

"They do if there's a mighty knight waving a magic sword in front of their noses," Howie snapped.

Eddie reached out and patted his friend on the back. "Don't get mad," Eddie said. "But there are no such things as dragons."

"I say there are," Howie yelled.

Eddie stood up straight and rolled his fingers into a tight fist. "I say there aren't," Eddie yelled back.

Melody stepped between her two friends. "There's only one way to prove whether dragons exist," she said.

"How?" Eddie and Howie asked.

"Meet me here after school, and I'll tell you," she said. "But beware. It may be dangerous. Very dangerous!"

# 8

# Fire-Breathing Trouble

"We'd better hurry or I'm going to get in trouble with my mom for being late," Liza complained as they walked to the bus stop.

"We'll all be in trouble if there really is a dragon," Melody said. "Fire-breathing trouble."

Eddie stopped at the bus stop and looked at his friends. "I don't mind going, because I'd rather do anything than my homework. But, I have to tell you, this whole thing is a waste of time."

"What if we can prove there really is a dragon?" Howie said as the city bus pulled up to the stop.

Eddie jumped on the bus and called back to his friends, "If you can prove there's a dragon, then I'll eat my dragon hat."

Howie, Eddie, Melody, and Liza didn't say another word until the bus bounced over some railroad tracks and pulled up in front of Jewel's Pizza Castle. As they piled off the bus, Liza whispered, "Now what are we going to do?"

"We can't just march in and demand to see their friendly neighborhood dragon," Howie said.

"I have an idea," Melody said. She raced around to the back of the building with her friends close behind. A huge green trash bin sat not far from the back door. Melody slid in behind the bin. Liza, Howie, and Eddie squeezed in with her.

"Phe-ew!" Eddie muttered. "What kind of slop did they put in this trash can? It stinks worse than cafeteria food."

Liza giggled. "Maybe it's dragon poop."

"Shhh," Howie hissed. "They'll hear us."

The four kids got quiet and watched the gray metal door to Jewel's Pizza Castle. Five minutes went by and nothing happened. Ten minutes went by.

"This is more boring than licking stamps," Eddie complained.

Just then the gray door swung open and a knight in shining armor swung a bag of garbage into the trash bin. Several pizza crusts fell out of the bag and landed with a thud on top of Eddie's head. The knight slammed the door as he went back inside.

Eddie stood up and knocked the pizza off his head. "This has to be the worst mess you've ever gotten me into," Eddie yelled at Melody. "I'm going home. I'd rather do my homework than be a human trash can."

"Go ahead," Howie told Eddie. "But you're going to miss all the fun. I'm going inside that dungeon and I'm going to find that dragon."

# 9

## Toast

"You're going to do what?" Liza squealed.

"I'm going inside the dungeon and I'm going to set that dragon free," Howie told them.

"Hold on just a minute," Melody said with her hands on her hips. "Have you ever thought about what Bailey City would be like if there was a dragon flying around?"

"Toasted Bailey City," Eddie snickered.

Liza put her hand on Howie's arm. "I hate to think of anything being kept captive. But maybe it's better this way. What if the dragon's still mean? He might try to eat us."

"Would you like to be chained to a

pizza oven for the rest of your life?" Howie asked.

Eddie laughed. "It'd be better than having to go to school. I'd have free pizza whenever I wanted."

"As long as you slaved over a hot oven cooking it," Howie reminded him.

"It couldn't be worse than two-digit multiplication," Eddie said.

Melody pointed to the door. "It doesn't matter," she said. "I bet that door is locked up tighter than a king's treasure."

"I'll see about that," Howie said. He eased around the trash bin and tiptoed toward the gray door.

"Don't do it," Liza called. Howie looked back and put his finger to his lips. Without a word, he pulled on the big silver handle.

"I can't believe it," Melody whispered. "It opened."

"I can't believe it, either," Eddie

pointed to the door. "Howie just went into the dungeon!"

"Hurry!" Liza screeched at Eddie. "You have to help him!"

"Me?" Eddie said. "I don't even believe there is a dragon. Why should I help Howie? He can get arrested for trespassing all by himself."

"I'm not worried about him getting arrested," Liza said. "I'm worried about him getting turned into french fries!"

"Pizza," Eddie corrected her. "This is a pizza joint. They don't serve fries."

"They'll be serving Howie on a plate if you don't help him," Liza said.

"Eddie's afraid," Melody snapped. "We'll have to save Howie ourselves." Melody grabbed Liza's arm and pulled her to the door.

"I'm not scared," Eddie said and followed Melody. Together the three friends disappeared inside the dungeon.

# 10

## Glowing

The kitchen was as dark as a cave. A single EXIT sign over the door cast a red glow in the cold, damp room. Dusty swords hung along the walls and a suit of armor was piled in one corner. A shield with a big red cross leaned against the suit of armor. Huge metal bowls were stacked on long silver tables. Every bowl was dirty and the tables had globs of pizza dough stuck to them.

"This place is a wreck," Eddie muttered.

Liza shivered. "I just hope Howie is okay."

"Where is he?" Melody asked. The three friends huddled together and walked away from the outside door. They were in the middle of the room when the door slammed shut with a loud bang!

"Trapped," Liza said with a gulp.

"Listen," Melody said. "I hear something." The three kids stood still and waited. In a second they heard it.

It was a low rumble. Then it got louder and louder. The metal bowls began to rattle and one fell onto the floor with a loud clang.

"Wh . . . what's happening?" Liza said.

"I think the dragon has Howie," Melody said.

"Look there!" Eddie hollered. He pointed to a big black hole at the side of the dungeon. Two glowing red eyes stared out at the kids and smoke bellowed from the darkness.

"It's the dragon!" Liza screamed.

Melody yelled, "Let's get out of here!" Melody, Liza, and Eddie ran from the dungeon into the dining area.

"Quick, head for the front door," Eddie said. Melody ran toward the door, but she bumped right into George instead.

# 11

# The Late Great Howie

George towered over the three kids. The tarnished suit of armor he wore made loud clanging noises. In one hand was a shield, and in the other he held a long shiny sword with a fancy handle. It was the same sword that had been hanging on the wall the day before.

"Out of my way," George bellowed. "My chef has a problem!"

Melody scooted out of the way and Liza ducked behind a chair. But Eddie planted his feet and refused to move.

"There is a BIG problem with your pizza chef," Eddie told George. "He ate our friend!"

George sat down in a chair with a heavy thump. "There must be some mistake," George sputtered. Just then, there

was a long, low rumble from the kitchen. It sounded exactly like a giant burp.

"Oh, no!" Liza cried. "Eddie's right. The dragon just gobbled a Howie-burger for lunch!"

"Dragon?" George asked in a whisper. "Who said anything about a dragon?"

"The late great Howie did," Melody blurted. "He figured it out from the riddle. But we didn't believe him."

"That's why he sneaked into your kitchen," Eddie said. "He was going to prove you had a dragon for a cook."

"Poor Howie," Liza said with a sniffle. "We should have believed him. Then he would still be alive."

Melody nodded. "Howie was always right."

"He was the smartest kid in all of Bailey City," Eddie added right before the dungeon door swung open and whacked him on the behind.

"I'm glad you think I'm smart," a familiar voice said. "I'll never let you forget you said that."

"Howie!" Melody, Liza, and Eddie yelled all at once. "You're alive!"

"Of course, I'm alive," Howie said. "I'm way too smart to be roasted by an ancient fire-breathing monster."

George let out a long breath and smiled. "See, your friend is fine and dandy," he said. "There is no dragon. So you can run along home."

"Not so fast," Howie told him as a deep rumble rattled the pictures on the wall. When it finally stopped, Howie tapped the center of George's chest. It made a hollow ringing sound on his armor. "You have some explaining to do," Howie told George.

George jumped to his feet and held up his sword. "Nonsense," he said. "I'm in charge here."

"You won't be in charge for long," Howie told George in his most grown-up voice, "unless you listen to me." Then Howie turned and disappeared back into the dingy dungeon. George rushed through the swinging doors after him.

Liza looked at Eddie and Melody. "We have to go in there," Liza told her friends.

Melody nodded and Eddie took a deep breath. But when Liza tried the door, it was locked.

# 12

## Grand Opening

For a week, Howie's friends had begged him to tell them what happened in the dungeon of Jewel's Pizza Castle. And for a week, Howie had kept his lips sealed tight. Now Howie, Eddie, Melody, and Liza stared at the newly reopened Jewel's Pizza Castle. The restaurant had been closed a week. Bright flags waved from the turrets and big banners hung in the windows announcing a grand opening.

The banners and flags weren't the only things different about the restaurant. The windows sparkled and a brand-new stone fence circled the backyard. The fence was so high, the Bailey School kids couldn't see over it. Freshly painted signs hung all over the fence. They said: DANGER: KEEP OUT.

"Are you sure it's safe to eat here?" Liza asked.

Howie nodded. "I'm positive."

"I am, too," Eddie said. "Because I don't believe there really was a dragon."

"Eddie's right," Melody said. "We didn't see the dragon because you locked the door to the kitchen."

"I had to," Howie said.

"Why?" Liza asked.

"Everyone knows dragons are shy," Howie told them. "Having all of us crowd around his cave would make him nervous."

"Did you actually see the dragon?" Eddie asked.

"Well . . . not exactly," Howie admitted. "It was too dark in that dungeon of a kitchen. And that's exactly what I told George.

"I read in a book that dragons hate the cold and dark," Howie continued. "They need sunshine. It keeps them from getting grumpy. That's why George's dragon growled so much. When I told George, he knew what he had to do."

"What?" Melody asked.

Howie grinned. "He had to clean up the kitchen and build a pen for his dragon. Now, our friendly neighborhood dragon can soak up sun rays on his day off."

"I think the only place dragons sunbathe is in fairy tales," Eddie decided. "And in Howie's imagination." Then Eddie pushed open the newly painted door to Jewel's Pizza Castle.

"Wow," Liza whispered. "This place looks great." Liza was right. Colorful paint covered the walls and bright lights shone on brand-new tables and chairs. Everything sparkled.

The restaurant was crowded, but George hurried over to the four friends. "Welcome," George said with a smile. "I have a special treat for you."

George led them to a table. Then he disappeared inside the swinging doors. He came back carrying a huge pepperoni pizza.

"My chef made this especially for you," George said. "Enjoy."

All the kids grabbed a slice of pizza. They were so busy eating that they didn't hear it at first. But when Liza took a break from gobbling pizza, she noticed it.

"Did you hear that?" Liza asked.

Her friends stopped chewing to listen. Melody nodded. "It sounds like a big cat getting a belly rub."

"No cat purrs that loudly," Eddie said. Then he reached out and grabbed George's arm. "What's that noise?" Eddie asked.

"That," George told him, "is the sound of a happy cook. What else did you think it was . . . a dragon?"

And then George threw back his head and laughed.

## About the Authors

**Debbie Dadey and Marcia Thornton Jones** have fun writing stories together. When they both worked at an elementary school in Lexington, Kentucky, Debbie was the school librarian and Marcia was a teacher. During their lunch break in the school cafeteria, they came up with the idea of the Bailey School Kids.

Debbie and her family live in Fort Collins, Colorado. Marcia and her husband still live in Kentucky.

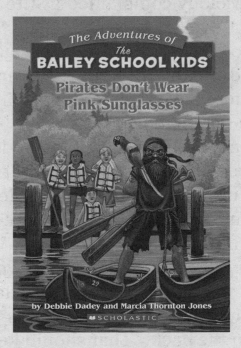

The Adventures of
The
BAILEY SCHOOL KIDS®
Pirates Don't Wear
Pink Sunglasses

by Debbie Dadey and Marcia Thornton Jones

SCHOLASTIC

# 1

## Mistletoe

"I can't believe we have to go back there," Melody complained as the school bus went over a bump.

Liza leaned her head out the bus window and moaned, "We'll never make it out of there alive. Mr. Jenkins will get us for sure this time."

The Bailey Elementary kids nodded as they remembered last summer at Camp Lone Wolf. They were sure Mr. Jenkins, their camp counselor, was a werewolf.

"He'll have to deal with me first," Eddie said from the seat behind the two girls. He held up a large clump of mistletoe.

"All right!" Howie slapped his friend Eddie on the back. "That should keep old werewolf-face in check." The kids had read in a book that people during the

Middle Ages used mistletoe to scare away werewolves.

Eddie stuffed the mistletoe into his blue Bailey City gym bag. "I still don't believe Mr. Jenkins is really a werewolf, but just in case. . . ."

"You're ready," Melody finished for him.

The four kids were silent as the bus passed the sign that said *Welcome to Camp Lone Wolf.* Tall weeds clung to the weathered sign. As the bus bumped over the gravel drive, Coach Ellison stood up in the front of the bus and grinned at the Bailey School kids.

"I always look forward to this nature trip," he said, rubbing his hands together. "Especially the boat race on Friday against the Sheldon Sharks."

"I don't know why," Liza mumbled. "Bailey School NEVER wins."

Melody nodded. "All we end up with are mosquito bites."

Every year the kids from Bailey Elementary went on a week-long nature trip. And every year the field trip ended with a rowing competition against the kids from nearby Sheldon City. The Bailey Boaters had never won a single race.

"But this time Coach Ellison says we're going to have a professional instructor," Howie told her.

"If Mr. Jenkins doesn't get us first." Melody shivered as she remembered Mr. Jenkins' wolf-like howls.

"Maybe Mr. Jenkins won't even be there," Liza said.

"Yeah, maybe he retired to the Old Werewolves' Home," Melody said hopefully.

Eddie shook his curly red head and pointed. "Not a chance. Look!"

As the bus squeaked to a stop, the four kids saw a very hairy Mr. Jenkins standing beside a picnic table. He wore no shoes, a brown Camp Lone Wolf T-shirt, and ragged blue jeans. Around his furry neck were silver dog tags. Beside him stood a stocky man with a long black beard and bright pink sunglasses. The stranger's frizzy black hair was tied back in a ponytail with a purple bandana, and a silver earring dangled from his left ear.

"Oh, no!" Melody gasped. "Now there's two of them!"

Howie gulped. "It's a werewolf convention."

"Everybody off!" Coach Ellison hollered from the front of the bus. "Let's get ready for those Sheldon Sharks!"

Liza followed her friends off the bus. "I just hope we don't get eaten first!"

# 2

## Captain Teach

"Welcome to Camp Lone Wolf, Bailey kids," Mr. Jenkins boomed in a voice loud enough to rattle the bus windows. "I hope you're ready to work those rowing muscles of yours."

"I hope he doesn't make a snack out of my muscles," Melody whispered, but she quickly fell silent when Mr. Jenkins glared at her. His eyes were bloodshot and underlined with dark circles. He looked like he hadn't slept since the last time she'd seen him.

"It's kind of you to give us a discount," Coach Ellison said. "The school couldn't afford to pay full price."

Mr. Jenkins scratched his tangled beard and shrugged. "Business has been slow. At least this way the camp is earning some money. And I was lucky to run into Captain Teach. He's helping out at no cost." Mr. Jenkins nodded to the burly man. "Teach knows all about making a crew shipshape, so you rookies pay attention and you'll win that boat race."

"I'd rather eat hot dogs and ice cream," Eddie laughed. But his smile faded when Mr. Jenkins grinned back, showing all his teeth.

Mr. Jenkins licked his lips. "We'll worry about eating later, after Teach is through with you."

Liza gulped. "I'm already worried."

"They're all yours," Mr. Jenkins told Captain Teach as he stalked into the woods.

Coach Ellison held his hand out to the new instructor. "Hello, I'm Frank Ellison, the Bailey coach." Instead of shaking his hand, Captain Teach spit on the dusty ground and adjusted his pink sunglasses.

Coach Ellison dropped his hand to his side and stammered, "We're honored to have an experienced instructor. Where did you get your experience?"

Captain Teach scowled and spoke with a gruff accent. "Me life has been the sea, and I work where the tide takes me." He winked at Coach Ellison and then turned to the kids clustered by the bus. "Why are you sailors loafing about?" he growled. "Get your gear stowed in the cabins and then hightail it to the docks. We've work to do."

The kids ran into each other as they grabbed their bags and headed for the cabins.

Melody, Liza, and the other girls dumped their bags on the bunks in Cabin Gray Wolf. Dust clouds poofed from the mattresses and made them sneeze. "This place is filthy," Melody snapped. "It looks like no one has been here since we left."

Liza knocked some cobwebs down with a pillow. "You're probably right. Everybody's started going to Camp Soaring Eagle on the other side of Sheldon City."

"Camp Soaring Eagle is fantastic," Carey said. "It's much better than this flea nest. It has horses, motor scooters, and even scuba gear. I went there for two weeks! It was a blast!" Carey's father was the president of the Bailey City bank, and she always got to do whatever she wanted. Most of the kids thought she was a brat.

"I don't think Camp Lone Wolf can afford that stuff," Liza said.

"It won't be able to afford to stay open if it doesn't do something fast," Carey snapped. "My dad said this place is broke. If they don't make this month's payment, Bailey Bank is going to take over."

"What does a bank want with a camp?" Melody asked.

Carey smiled. "They're going to sell it

to Mega-Mall Development Company so Bailey City can have the biggest mall in the country."

"But we already have a mall," Melody reminded Carey.

Liza looked out the dusty window at all of the tall pine trees. "It'd be a shame to tear down all those trees. And what about the animals and Mr. Jenkins?"

Carey shrugged. "Who cares about that mangy man and all those nasty creatures? A mall would be great!"

"I'm not so sure," Liza muttered as the girls headed back outside.

They met Eddie and Howie outside Cabin Silver Wolf. Tall weeds sprouted around the cabin. "This place is a mess," Howie said.

"It's gone to the dogs," Eddie laughed. "Or should I say the wolves?"

Liza's face turned pale. "Maybe wolves have taken over. After all, I haven't seen any other camp counselors."

"Liza's right," Melody said.

Eddie laughed at his friends. "I have plenty of mistletoe with me. Besides, Coach Ellison and Captain Teach are here. We have nothing to worry about."

Howie took a deep breath and looked at his friend. "I hope you're right."